Potato Pride

by Carol Domblewski
illustrated by Todd Leonardo

HOUGHTON MIFFLIN   BOSTON

No one loves potatoes more than fifteen-year-old Kate Lester. She eats mashed potatoes and baked potatoes. Her all-time favorite is French fries. But when fall comes, Kate groans at the thought of potatoes. That's because all she does, from morning till night, is dig them up.

Kate lives in Grand Isle, Maine. Her town is at the northern tip of the state, in Aroostook [uh-ROOS-tuk] County. In October, high schools in the county close for as long as three weeks. This lets students like Kate help with the potato harvest.

Kate would be the first to admit that this school break is not as great as it might sound. Harvesting potatoes is hard work.

Potatoes have been a part of life in this area of Maine for generations. In fact, potatoes are Maine's biggest crop. When harvest time rolls around, people take it very seriously. Most farmers harvest the potatoes using big machines. Kate's family is different.

On their farm, Kate's family grows three kinds of potatoes. One kind is the fingerling potato. It is small and tasty, and people love its size, color, and flavor. But not everyone knows about it, and few grocery stores sell it. It is a special kind of potato known as an heirloom potato. Heirlooms are things that have been handed down from one generation to the next.